Penny & Jelly

The School Show

Written by **Maria Gianferrari**   Illustrated by **Thyra Heder**

HOUGHTON MIFFLIN HARCOURT

Boston New York

For Anya, whose creativity is an
inspiration, and for her sweet dog sister,
Becca—best friends!   —M.G.

For my two favorite animals,
Jordan and Toby.   —T.H.

Text copyright © 2015 by Maria Gianferrari
Illustrations copyright © 2015 by Thyra Heder

www.hmhco.com

The text of this book is set in ITC Clearface.
The illustrations are watercolor, pencil and ink.

Library of Congress Cataloging-in-Publication Data
Gianferrari, Maria.
Penny and Jelly : the school show / written by Maria Gianferrari ;
and illustrated by Thyra Heder.
pages cm
Summary: As the talent show nears, Penny and her
trusty canine companion Jelly scramble to find Penny's talent.
ISBN 978-0-544-23014-9
[1. Talent shows—Fiction. 2. Dogs—Fiction. 3. Friendship—Fiction.]
I. Heder, Thyra, illustrator. II. Title. III. Title: School show.
PZ7.G339028Pe 2015
[E]—dc23
2014009670

Manufactured in China | SCP 10 9 8 7 6 5 4 3 2 1
4500524478

The Peabody Elementary School Talent Show was an annual tradition.

All of Penny's classmates were participating.

Some were singing.

Some were dancing.

Some were singing *and* dancing.

Penny could neither sing nor dance.

She had to find a talent. And fast.

With Jelly's help, Penny made a list of her top five talents:

1. Tuba playing
2. Juggling
3. Yodeling
4. Baton twirling
5. Jump roping

One by one, Penny crossed things off her list.

1. ~~Tuba playing~~

2. ~~Juggling~~

3. ~~Yodeling~~

4. ~~Baton twirling~~

5. ~~Jump roping~~

"I have to find a talent," said Penny.
"Ruff-roo-roo," barked Jelly.

"Ooh! I'll be a doggy fashion designer," said Penny, "and you'll be my model!"

PENNY

BEWARE OF DOG!

Penny rooted through her drawers.

She cut.

She tied.

She painted.

She pasted.

VOILÀ!

Jelly shook.

Jelly jiggled.

Jelly rolled.

Riiiip.

"Where am I going to find a talent?" said Penny.

"Ruff-roo-roo!" barked Jelly.

"Ooh! I'll be a ballroom dancer," said Penny, "and you'll be my partner!"

Penny tried to foxtrot,
but her foot got caught.

Penny tried to jive
and took a nosedive.

Penny tried to cha-cha,
but Jelly said "See ya!"

"I need a talent *now!*"
said Penny.

"Ruff-roo-roo!" barked Jelly.
"Ooh! I'll be a magician—
the Amazing Penny," said Penny,
"and you'll be my trusty assistant!"

Penny pulled Jelly out of a hat.
Sort of.

Penny sawed Jelly in half.
Kind of.

Penny made Jelly disappear.

Alacazam!

Abracadabra!

poof!

Shazam!

Not.

8. Magician

"I'll never find a talent in time!" said Penny.

Penny made list

9. ~~Bubblegum blowing~~
10. ~~Toe snapping~~
11. ~~Unicycle riding~~

after list

12. ~~Ear wiggling~~
13. ~~Drum playing~~
14. ~~Plate balancing~~

after list . . .

15. ~~Stilt walking~~
16. ~~Eye crossing~~
17. ~~Snake charming~~

until everything was crossed off.

Penny climbed into her closet with Jelly. If she hid, she could skip the talent show. No one at school would witness her Untalentedness.

"Ruff-roo-ROO!" barked Jelly.
"ROO to you too," said Penny.

roo ROOO!

"Roo-ROO," answered Jelly.

"Ooh!" said Penny.

"I know what we'll do!"

ROO!
ROOO!

That night, the drumroll sounded.

Penny blew her kazoo:
"Wooooo."

And Jelly sang her dog duet.
"Roo-ROOO-ROOOO!"

WOO WOO!

WOO WOOO!

roo ROOO!

ROO ROOO!

They were not in tune.
But their duet had harmony.

Later, Principal MacGillicuddy
announced the winners.

But the best award of all went
to Penny and Jelly.